d e f g

l m n

r s t

x y z

6 7 8 9 10

THE BIG a b c AND COUNTING BOOK

compiled by LYNNE J BRADBURY
illustrated by LYNN N GRUNDY

This very colourful and boldly drawn book will give all young children a delightful introduction to the alphabet and numbers up to ten.

The alphabet section is completely phonetic, that is, each object begins with the *sound* of the letter (a as it sounds in apple) and not the *name* of the letter (a as it sounds in able). This will help children when they begin to read. The matching and recognition pages will reinforce children's ability to distinguish between different letter shapes.

The counting section introduces numbers, using familiar objects and gives practice in matching, sorting and counting.

All the pages have been carefully designed to achieve a purpose and simple sentences or questions will direct the child throughout the book. However, there is much more on each page which the child can look at and talk about. An adult can draw attention to all sorts of other topics, such as colour, shape and size and explain anything unfamiliar.

0 7214 7506 X

alphabet

a

arrow

apple

axe

alligator

Aa

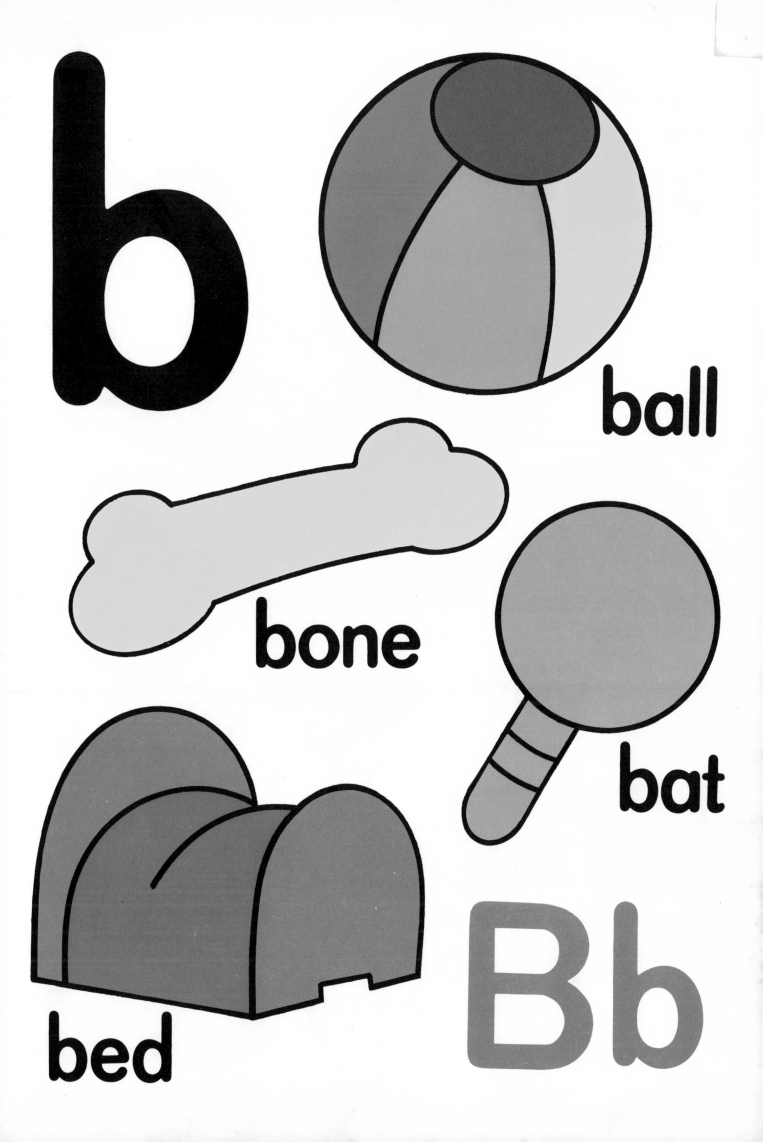

b

ball

bone

bat

bed

Bb

C

cat

car

comb

cup

Cc

d

dinosaur

diver

dog

Dd

e

elephant

eskimo

egg

Ee

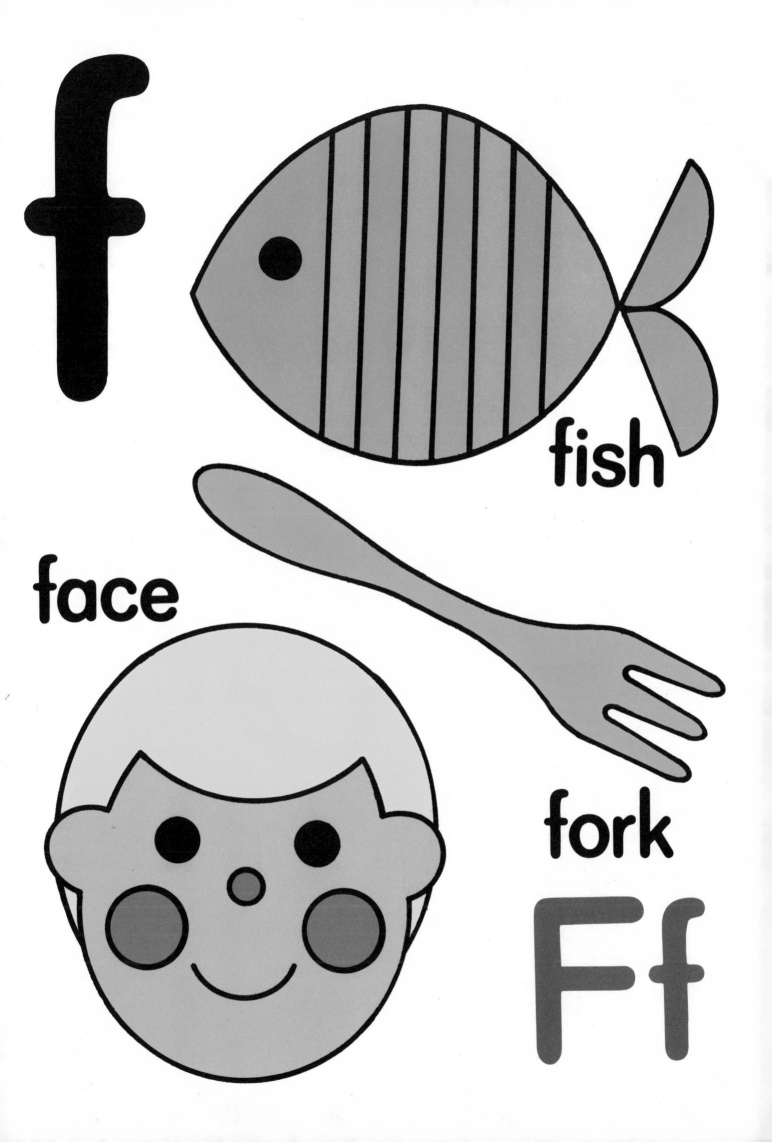

f

fish

face

fork

Ff

goat

gun

gate

Gg

h

house

hammer

hat

hedgehog

Hh

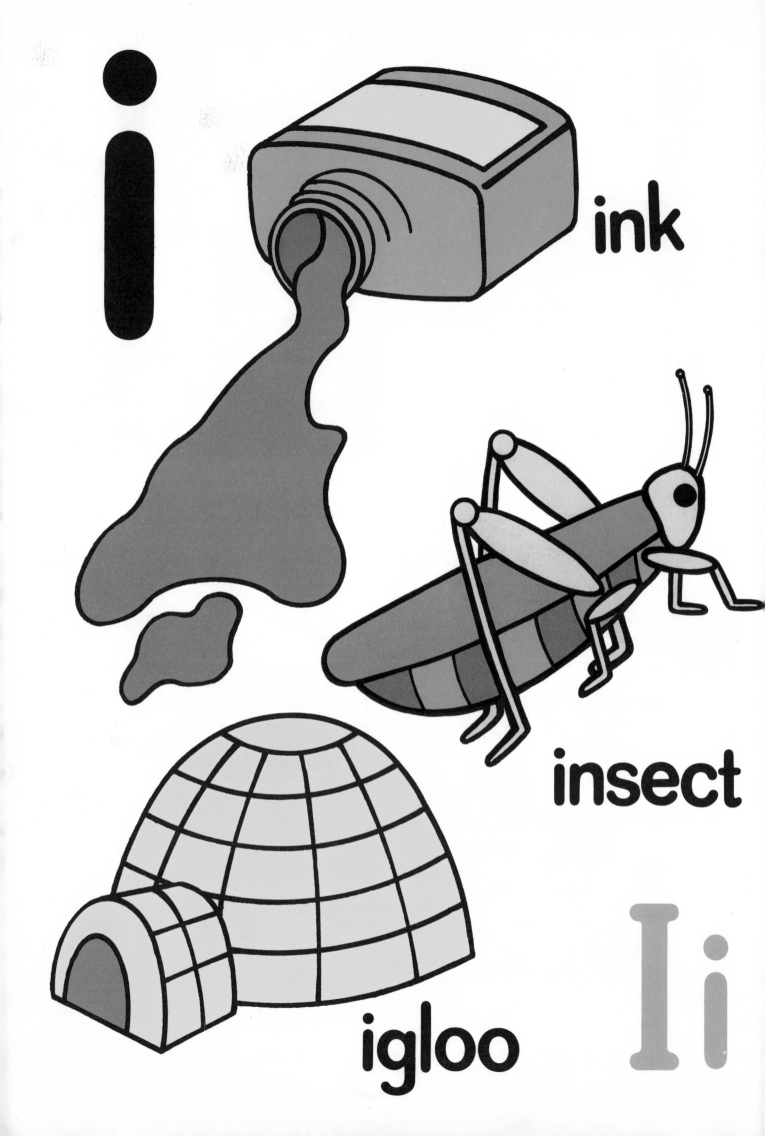

i

ink

insect

igloo

Ii

j

jelly

jug

jam
jar

Jj

k

kite

key

kangaroo

Kk

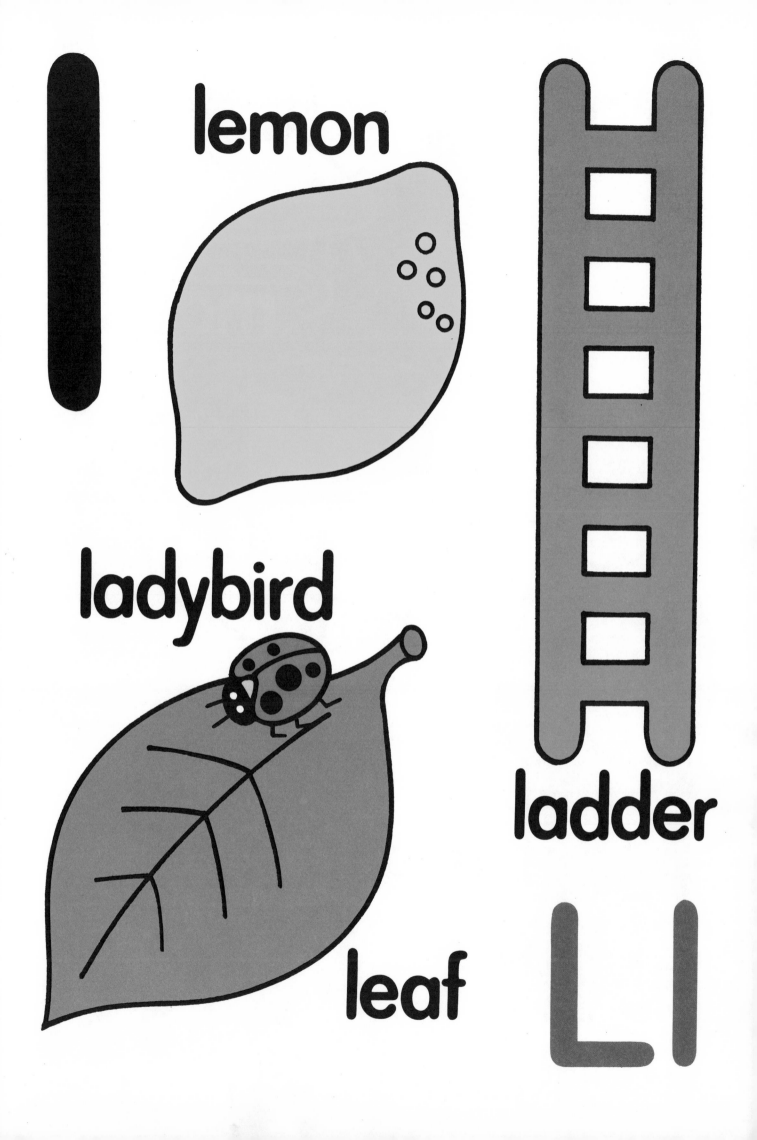

lemon

ladybird

ladder

leaf

Ll

m

mouse

mug

moon

man

Mm

nurse

net

nail

Nn

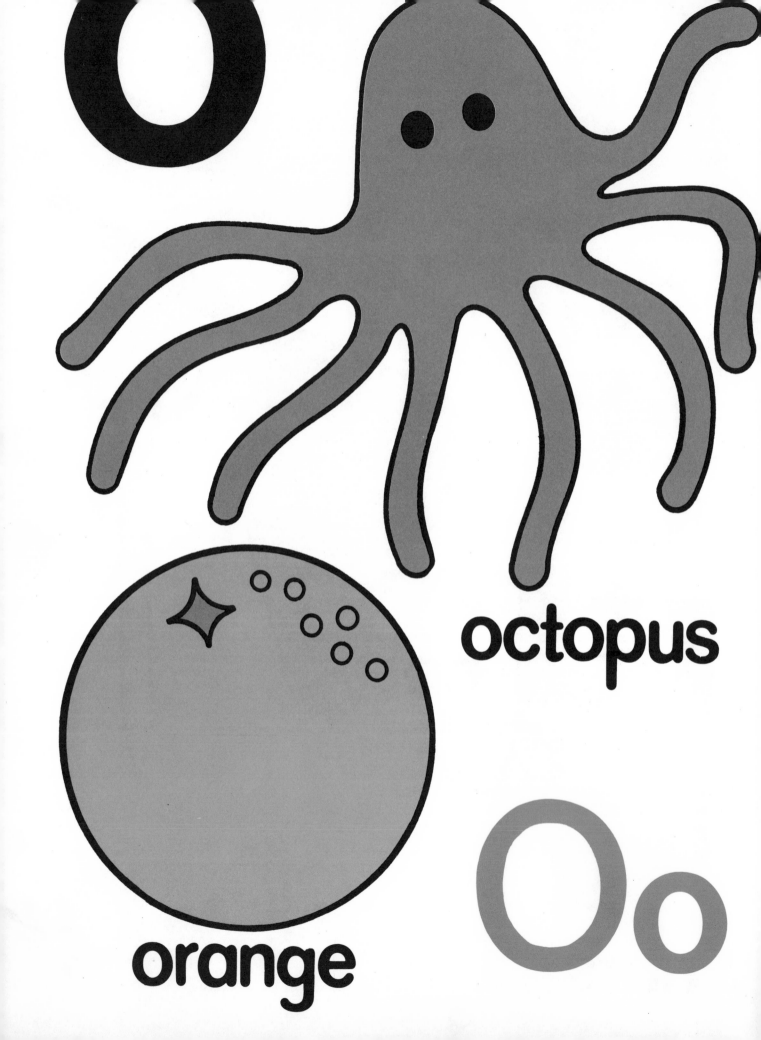

O

octopus

orange

Oo

p

parrot

peg

pig

Pp

q

quads

queen

Qq

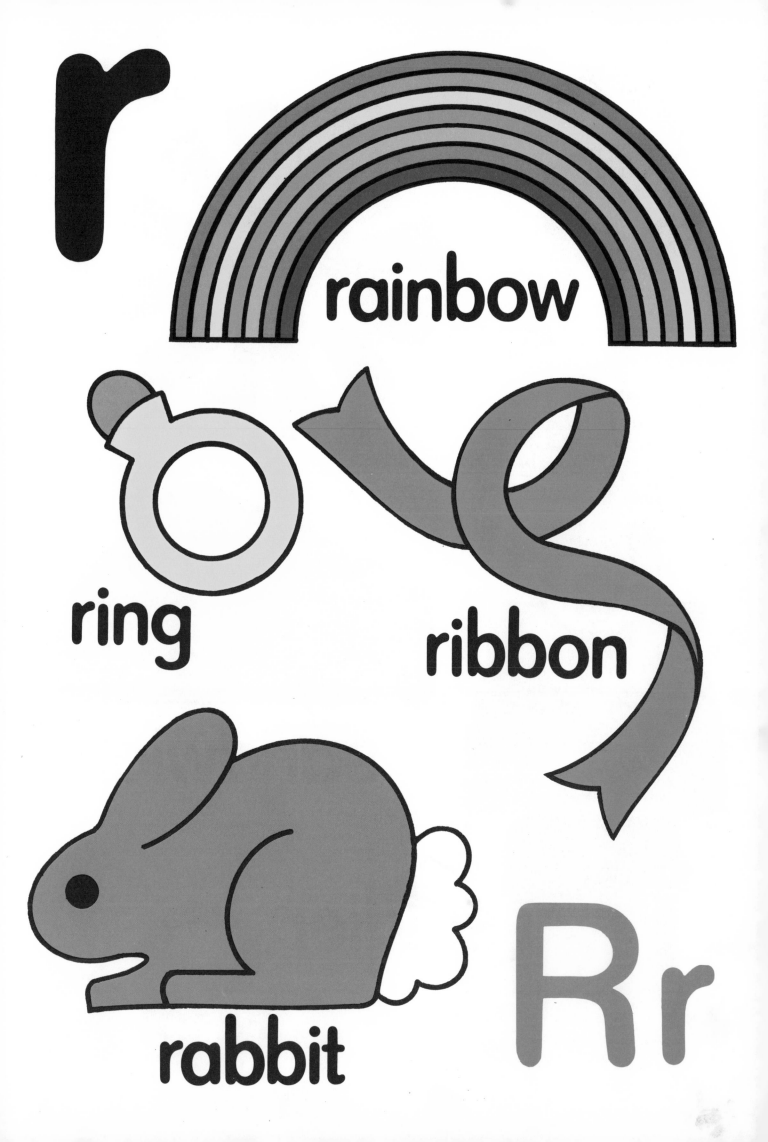

r

rainbow

ring

ribbon

rabbit

Rr

S

sun

sandwich

soldier

Ss

t

tortoise

tomato

television

T t

u

umbrella

umpire

Uu

V violin

van

volcano

Vv

window

wellingtons

watch

Ww

x ray

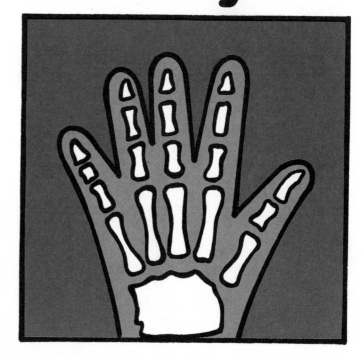

x as in box

x as in fox

Xx

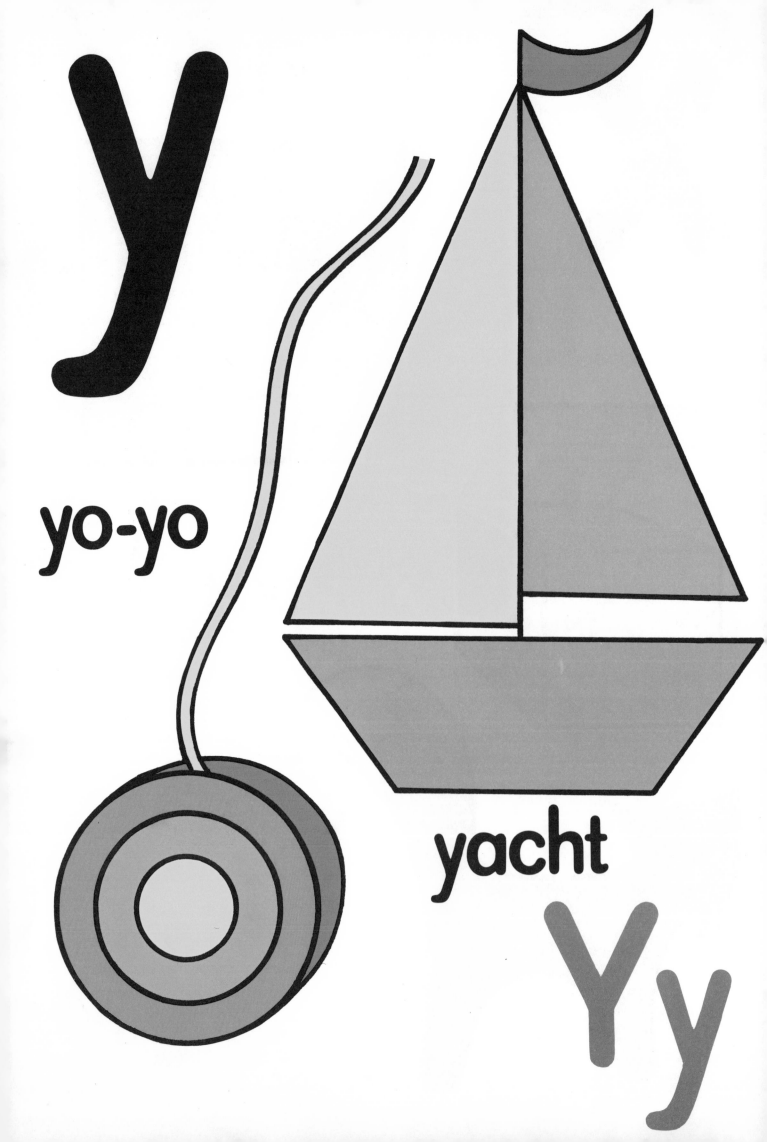

y

yo-yo

yacht

Yy

Z

zebra

zip

Zz

Can you name these?
What sound does each one start with?

Look back in the book to see if you are right.

Which letters go together?

t g q

i m a

b d r

AMT

GQI

RBD

Look back in the book to see if you are right.

Find another letter

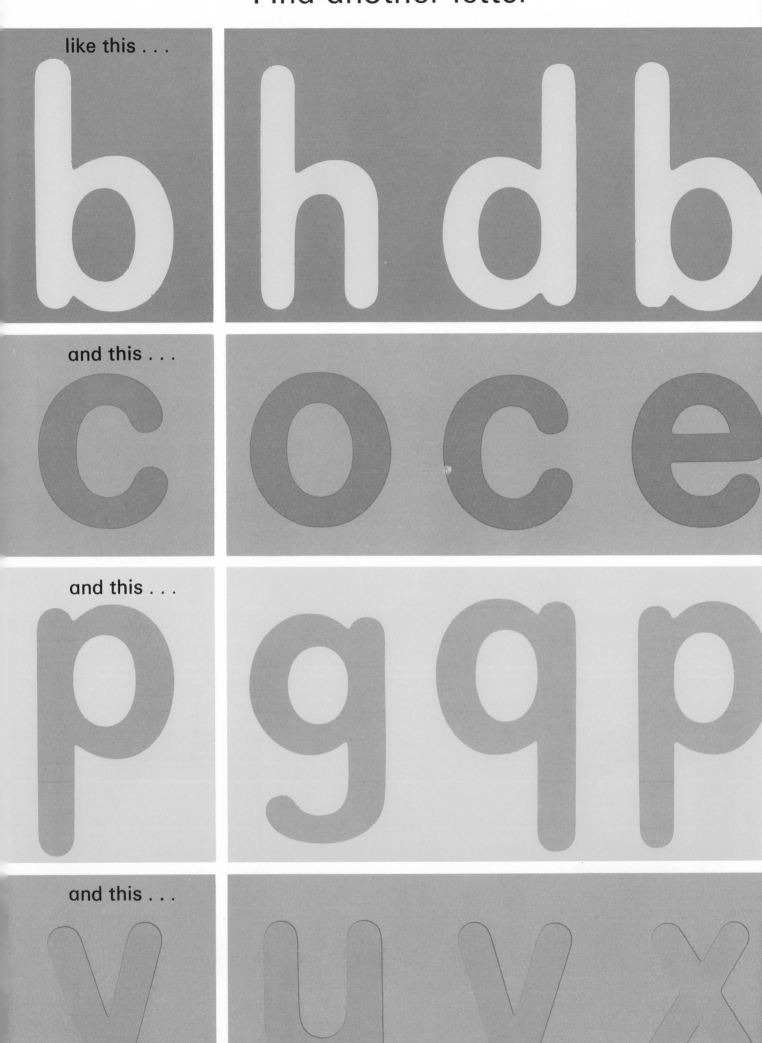

like this . . .

b h d b

and this . . .

c o c e

and this . . .

p g q p

and this . . .

v u v x

counting

1 one

1 frog

2 two

2 soldiers

3 three

3 teddy bears

4 four

4 mugs

5 five

5 eggs

6 six

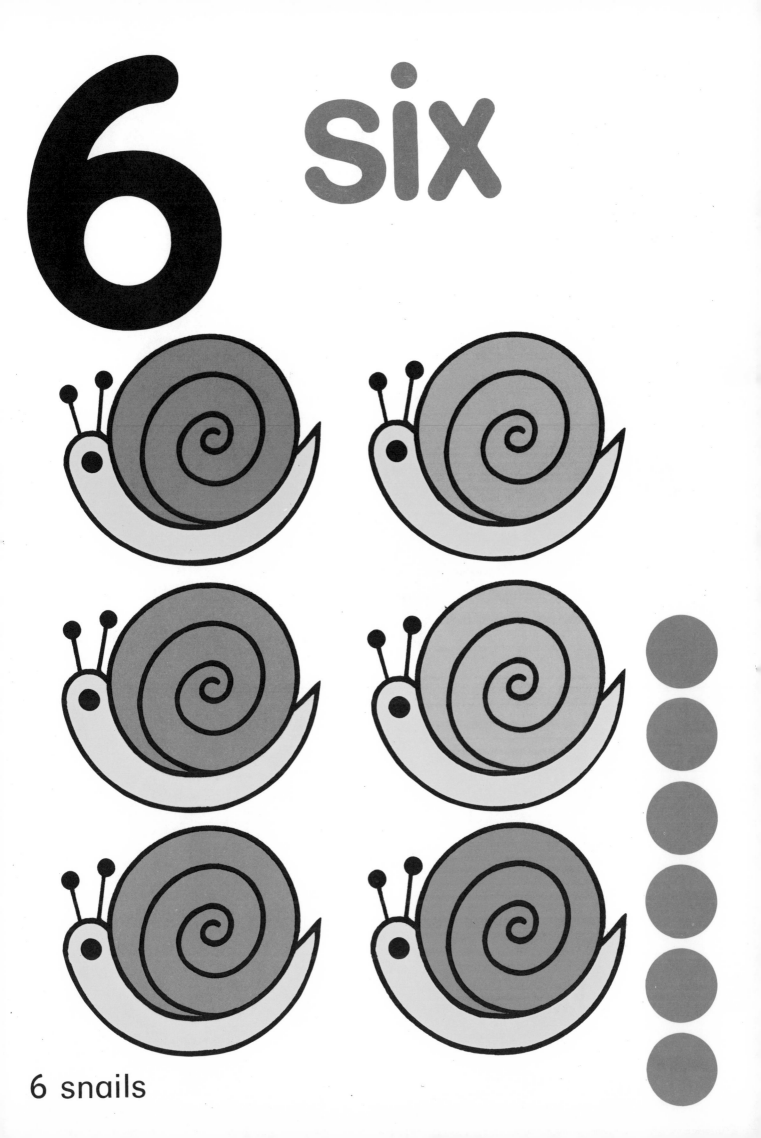

6 snails

7 seven

7 butterflies

8 eight

8 balls

9 nine

9 ladybirds

10 ten

10 buttons

How many houses can you count?

Does the milkman have one bottle of milk for each house?

Count the windows
on each house.

Does the baker
have one loaf of bread
for each house?

Count how many things go into the stew.

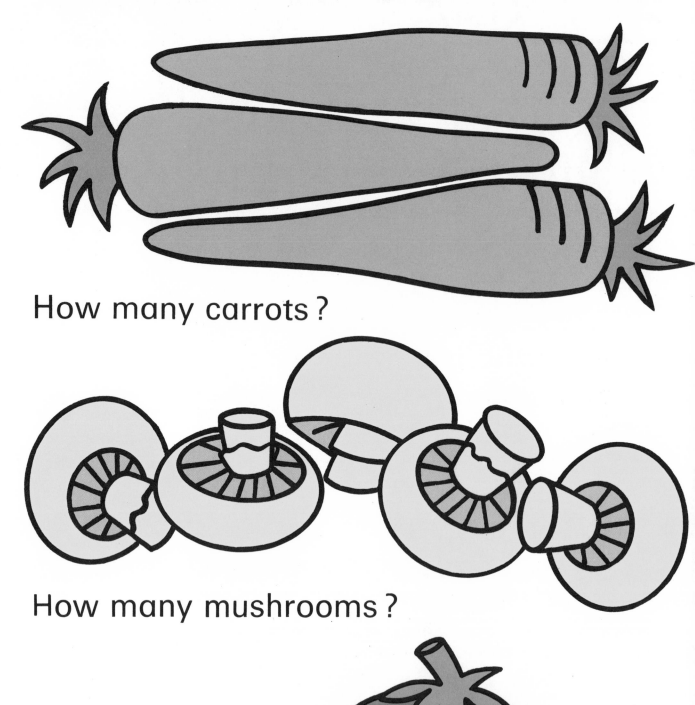

How many carrots ?

How many mushrooms ?

How many tomatoes ?

How many peas?

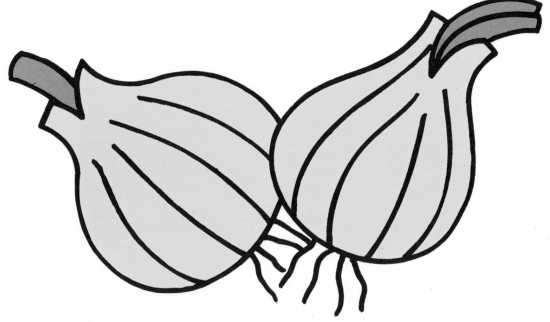

How many onions?

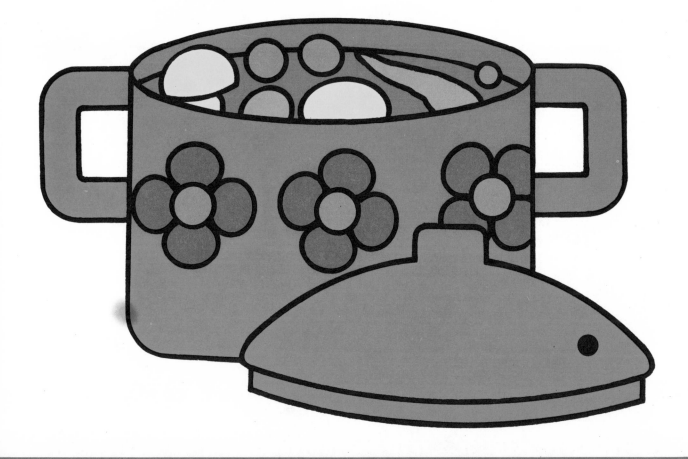

Count going down

10 9 8 7 6 5 4 3 2 1

10 9 8 7 6 5 4 3 2 1

Count going up

How many balls can the clown juggle with?
Which ball is different?

If he drops one, how many are left?
Count the spots on the clown's trousers.

All these numbers are **odd** numbers.

1

3

5

7

9

All these numbers are **even** numbers.

2

4

6

8

10

Count how many buttons on the giant's shirt.

How many blue buttons are there?
How many red buttons?

Say the numbers on the blue buttons.
These are **odd** numbers.

Do you know the numbers for the red buttons?
These are **even** numbers.

Look back in the book to see if you are right.

How many animals are at the bus stop ?

1st	2nd	3rd	4th	5th
first	second	third	fourth	fifth

Which animal is third ?

6th
sixth

7th
seventh

8th
eighth

9th
ninth

10th
tenth

Who has to wait until last?

a b c

h i j k

o p q

u v w

1 2 3 4 5